Plumply, Dumply Pumpkin

Plumply, Dumply Pumpkin

written by Mary Serfozo

illustrated by Valeria Petrone

Margaret K. McElderry Books

New York London Toronto Sydney Singapore

Also by Mary Serfozo

WHAT'S WHAT? A GUESSING GAME
illustrated by Keiko Narahashi

WHO SAID RED?
illustrated by Keiko Narahashi

Margaret K. McElderry Books

An imprint of Simon & Schuster Children's Publishing Division

1230 Avenue of the Americas

New York, New York 10020

Book design by Kristin Smith

The text for this book is set in Jam Loud.

The illustrations are digitally rendered.

Manufactured in China

1216 SCP

4 6 8 10 9 7 5

Library of Congress Cataloging-in-Publication Data

Serfozo, Mary.

Plumply, dumply pumpkin / written by Mary Serfozo ; illustrated by Valeria Petrone—1st ed.

p. cm.

Summary: Peter finds the perfect pumpkin so that he and his dad can make a jack-o-lantern.

ISBN 978-0-689-83834-7

[1. Pumpkin—Fiction. 2. Jack-o-lanterns—Fiction. 3. Stories in rhyme.] I. Petrone, Valeria, ill. II. Title.

PZ8.3.S4688 PI 2001

[E]—dc21

00-032421

To Julie Dahlen,
a "real" librarian
—M. S.

Peter's looking for a pumpkin,
a perfect plumply, dumply pumpkin.

Not a lumpy, bumpy pumpkin.

Not a stumpy, grumpy pumpkin,
but a sunny, sumptuous pumpkin.

Finally on a twining vine
he spies a pumpkin fat and fine!

Not too fat, though, not at all.
Not too short and not too tall.

Not some squat, lopsided pumpkin,
but a glossy lot of pumpkin.

Why does Peter want a pumpkin?

Want a showy, glowy pumpkin?

Pumpkin pickles?
Pumpkin pie?

Pumpkin pudding?
Pumpkin fry?

Pumpkin salad?
Pumpkin stew?

What is Peter going to do?

With his pumpkin home at last,

Peter starts in working fast.

Draws some eyes and draws a chin,
then draws a plumply, dumply grin.

Helps his dad carve into place
a simply dimply, dumply face.

Lights a light behind the grin
to start it glowing from within.

Later wins the most applause.
And really no surprise because . . .

Perfect pumpkins really do make perfect jack-o-lanterns, too.